ANIMALS
OF THE EXODUS

Alexander Zelenyj

Animals of the Exodus

by Alexander Zelenyj

ISBN: 978-1-908125-835

Cover Art by David Rix

Publication Date: July 2019

All text copyright 2019 Alexander Zelenyj

A different version of the story "The Mayflies Want to Fly" was originally
published in *Underground Voices, Volume 3* (2008) as "The June Bugs Want
to Fly".

CONTENTS

TAKING KAREN AWAY

Karen beneath him, squirming and trembling and choking with his fingers gripping her soft throat the way some men held guns and grenades and other un-beautiful things. He squeezed tighter and she gave him the muted song of her whimpering and breathing stoppered under his strength.

Around them, wildflowers nodded in the gentle breeze. In the trees marking the perimeter of the glade, nightbirds sang. Overhead, the twin stars of Sirius blazed like living miracles of godly genius, overseeing the rituals of all the tiny animals beneath them.

Tears were streaming from her eyes, catching the gibbous moon's light like evidences of a nocturnal spell. Her fingers clenched his bare arms, her nails bit and bled him. With arched back and neck offered she looked like an alabaster idol sculpted for his worship. He wept too.

Slowly, the walls began their forming around them, growing from a phantom impression haunting the air to a more translucent permanence; softening the moonlight; hiding them more completely.

One hand still gripping her windpipe, he let go with the other and made it into a fist ready to kiss her.

This was love. This was the secret Paradise hidden amid the world's great weights. This was the impregnable fortress whose walls were erected through the ritual of their union. He'd never known it before Karen. He gave himself up to the moment, to her. His heart hammered its joy to the world, in perfect percussion alongside her ecstatic voice escaping his Herculean grip and rising moonwards:

Thank . . . you.
Thank . . . you.
Thank you!

When they woke the sun was out. It coloured the glade a bright and warm and normal and un-demoned place. It was quiet, in the hushed hour before the crickets were awake to greet the new day, far away from the city murmuring like a dark dream in the west.

The fortress walls had begun their fading, as they always did, the lush vegetation of black oaks now visible through their shimmering translucence. They knew they had to cherish these final and dying moments of the miracle-place they'd made together before the new day was fully upon them.

They held each other in the luxurious silence, conscious of the other's wakefulness but wise enough to not ruin their remarkable peace with the hardness of words. But he wanted her to know that he lived to serve her: he kissed the necklace of bruises around her throat.

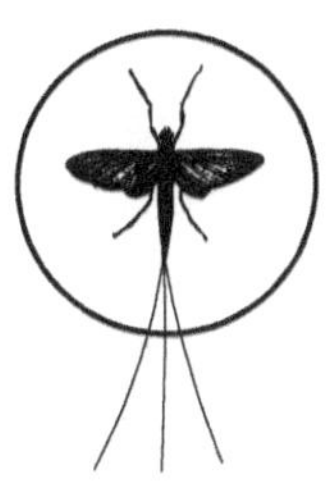

CELESTE
HAD TO GO AWAY

"There is a place."

The words escaped her in a breathless whisper even as her heart erupted into a frenzied hammering and tears filled her eyes, making a silver smear of the vision that was materialized before her like a long-recurring dream come to miraculous life.

There they were, the way she'd imagined so many times, taking to the tiny makeshift wooden stage that had been erected in their honour by unknown hands, dwarfing it with the sheer spectacle of their alien presence; with the overwhelming aura which knowledge of who they were brought with them:

The Deathray Bradburys.

Each of the five group members appeared, seemingly materializing from among the trees that bordered nearly flush against the rear of the stage. They were clad in the silver bodysuits for which they were known, like actors from a 1950s science fiction film, the meager string of holiday light bulbs overhanging the stage reflecting from them and throwing refractions in all directions; masked, silver-winged, antennae waving on the humid air, silver goggles gleaming as they picked up their instruments and turned to survey the crowd of forty people gathered in the field.

Their disciples cried out at the sight of them, their voices ecstatic and electric in the night. The band stood out starkly against the dark wall of black oaks rearing behind them, shimmering like apparitions in the uncertain light. The guitar player touched a knob on his silver instrument and a wave of feedback erupted from the silver-painted amplifier to roll across the crowd.

She laughed a laugh of pure joy. Tears continued to pour from her eyes.

It was happening.

It was all true.

The prophecy was *real*.

They'd *returned*.

Their story, as Biblically fantastical as it seemed to the many non-believers Celeste had heard speak out against them, was in that incredible moment confirmed. All the rumors in the underground papers in the preceding months had been true too: they *had* chosen this obscure town, on this particular late-summer night, for this extraordinary event, as in the past they'd often chosen similarly unexceptional towns on the outskirts of bigger cities for their legendary gatherings.

And here they were, ten years after their initial disappearance, once again bringing salvation to those who needed it.

And here *she* was, among the worthy.

"I love you always, Celeste."

She turned at the words, shouted into her ear over the pulsating waves of feedback. There were tears in her father's eyes as he smiled down at her. He was a good man, the best dad she could have asked for.

It was he that had heard about this night, and the return of the mythical punk rock group; and, amazingly, it was he who'd told her about it. Seeing her obsession over the course of the past year – the strength she got from the music created by this mysterious collective, from the words of their songs and what it all meant when taken together in relation to the thing she'd been going through – had compelled him to begin his digging. And his research had unearthed a deep history indeed, meaningful beyond the surface-level attention and infamy the group had gained through what so many people saw as a suicide cult's mission of bringing deadly salvation to its followers. He'd seen that there was so much more to it than that.

She'd watched him delve deeper, discovering the band's mission as obsessively explained through the lyrics of their songs, through the dense and literate liner notes that accompanied their single album and many 45s, and the literature in the pamphlets distributed at their concerts – their quest to fulfill a cosmic destiny of finding those who've suffered irrepairable trauma, and taking them away from the place of their suffering to a distant Paradise: the binary star, Sirius.

She'd told him about the zealous devotion of the fans who, like her, treated the band as liberators and their proposed mythology as absolute and unequivocal reality, unlike any relationship between artist and fans elsewhere. She'd shown him copies of the underground fanzine, *Burning Twins*, devoted to discussions of and tributes to the band – and after a fruitless search in their town's bookstores, he'd located a copy of the newest issue at a music shop, stuffed amid a slew of glossy magazines in a steel rack. It was in this issue that he'd read the article claiming that the Deathray Bradburys had returned, and were to perform once again, here, in this remote, sleepy and unremarkable Ontario town of old farmhouses and fields upon fields of wheat and corn and scarecrows and haze.

He understood her and had given her everything he could, even if her mother didn't agree with this. Not everyone could have faith in such fantastical tales. Not everyone believed.

He leaned to her and kissed her head. Then he turned abruptly, and was disappeared from the salty wash of her vision, just as the singer's voice rose above the feedback screaming across the fields:

"Good evening, friends."

The crowd roared louder, wept uncontrollably, hands reaching toward him. He stood there, silver and resplendent surveying his followers.

"We thank you for finding us, after all the long hard years you have endured. But know this, my friends: none of it was your fault. And yes, it *has* been far too long, but we have returned for you, and on this night we shall leave this scarred place and return to the Paradise among the stars, along with the most worthy of our followers . . ."

Here he raised his silver-gloved hands high on the air to take in the crush of people before him.

She felt it in the screaming wall of sound feedbacking from the amplifiers, felt it in that voice addressing them – addressing *her*! – so familiar from the countless hours she'd worshipped within the sheltering temple of its message; those sacred hours locked inside her bedroom, headphones clamped over her ears as the music drowned her in its bottomless depths; so comforting; so ineffably beautiful; so *strong*, that warm sonic bath. And now, on this incredible and fateful night, it filled her completely. And then she felt it, and though she knew that most people in the world could never understand it or believe her if she tried to explain it to them, there was only one way to articulate the truth of what was happening in that moment:

A door was opening.

The singer's voice echoed across the crowd, the moon-washed night field:

"Are you ready, my children?"

Was she ready? Could she leave it all behind? All the badness that had sullied the goodness of her family and home life? Yes, yes of course she could. She had her father's blessing, and the blessing of the silver ones to whose temple she'd travelled, the only great pilgrimage of her seventeen years in the world.

She turned, seeking her father, her emotions a brew of fear and excitement and unbridled joy, but he was gone, lost among the bodies pressing close, having left her to be swallowed by the goodness pulsing from all around; like an inverted dream-world to the nightmare that had swallowed her over one year before, and that had pushed her past the edge of sanity and tolerance and strength. She thought of the ordeal now, and found that she was able to smile a grim smile as she stood there at the threshold of her imminent salvation.

She'd been missing for three days. She'd shared the details of those 72 hours like lifetimes endured in Hell with only the police, and her parents, and her most treasured childhood friend, the time-yellowed plush winged horse she'd named Flyer which she dug out from her closet the day she returned from the hospital; no one else knew what she'd endured, and even those few she'd told could never truly know. She'd found herself still remembering things, details that became suddenly exhumed from the deep place she'd automatically interred them. Now, though, she felt a new strength while looking into this grave of entombed memories; now, she felt brave again; now, she felt free.

"My heart is yours!"

Celeste turned at the emotion-wracked cry, close to her ear: the boy beside her looked about her age, sixteen or seventeen and eyes filled to brimming with the rapture she felt filling herself. The boy sensed her appraisal and turned to her, and must have seen in her eyes what she saw so clearly in his: and he smiled and threw an arm around Celeste's shoulders, holding her like a brother as the noise continued to crash over them all like surging waves sculpting a shoreline. The boy was taller than she, and as he leaned close Celeste saw a string of words inked into the skin of his neck in a clumsy scrawl, undoubtedly his own:

There is a place.

A familiar and beloved snippet of song lyrics; a poem; a promise. Yes, she was in the right place on this night. She'd found her tribe.

A light, bright and ineffable, seemed to have begun pulsing, stronger than the scant stage lights. It came from the band, from the sky, from the grass beneath their feet, from inside each of them.

Celeste blubbered, all shame gone as she gave herself up to feeling like a child again and offered her voice into the roar, another essential ingredient in the rite being enacted: "Thank you, dad – I love you, dad."

As if replying directly to her, the singer's invincible voice of comfort was everywhere again:

"We are the Deathray Bradburys, and tonight is a celebration. Tonight is the festival of your salvation!"

She joined those around her in crying out at this, inarticulately, primal – hearing those words of welcome drove home the reality of their shared, long-sought dream.

On the light-washed stage, the bass player stepped to his silver microphone. He shouted a frantic count-in:

"1-2-3-4!"

The roar of the convened followers rose higher to meet the beautiful cacophony that erupted from the stage.

The ritual was begun.

The door – closed for so long to those broken souls gathered there that night – finally was flung wide.

In the aftermath of the performance, a great silence lay over the field, and a sleepy confusion hung over the handful of those left behind.

These people milled at the edge of the field, blinking or rubbing at their eyes, coming up from the heavy weariness that had settled over them as if waking from dreams. They grew slowly aware that there were much fewer people present than had been there before the performance had begun an hour earlier (or had it been much, much longer ago than this?). Indeed, as they looked about themselves, they understood that the main body of people who'd been there was gone: their loved ones; sons, daughters, brothers, sisters, best friends.

One old man was crying where he stood, clutching the photograph of a granddaughter that no longer stood on the field, swaying to the music of a band that had touched her in a way he'd never been cursed to understand. A ways from him a woman was kneeling on the grass, crying quietly, eyes riveted on the vault of the night sky. Through her tears, voice trembling, she said: "My sister – she's with you now – please take care of her."

Several people followed where she looked and found the twin stars burning conspicuously brighter than all the rest, pulsing like proof of something incredible beyond what they knew.

The night belonged to their loved ones, the departed; but it belonged to them, too. They, the unbroken, who'd helped the others make good their escape.

One man remained standing among the shadows thrown by the trees fringing the field while the others dispersed, returned to their vehicles, drove off into the night. He continued looking out across the moon-silvered grass and the now-empty stage. His voice was low as he spoke into the battered and archaic cellular phone at his ear.

"It's me."

A pause, the tinny voice of his wife on the opposite end of the line two provinces away frantic and buzzing in the stillness.

He said, "I did. She's gone."

Again her tinny voice, higher and more panicked, a fly-like buzzing and shrieking.

"That's fine. You can hate me all you need to. I did what I did for Celeste. Out of love. And compassion. Because . . . because she had to go away. She *had* to. You know this, Maria. In your heart, I know you know this."

He swallowed back tears, and listened to the heavy silence in the phone, interrupted by crackles of distance, and a fizzing of white noise.

A minute passed. His wife's voice began to weep inside the phone. An owl grumbled moodily from the darkness of the branches above him. Miles away, the baying of a dog came from the houses beyond the forest, sounding wild, undomesticated. Maybe it was a coyote, he thought distantly. The wind blew, unseasonal and cold, heralding coming Fall.

Then:

A brilliant light pulsed overhead, blinding, and without accompanying sound of any kind. Its arrival was so sudden, its brightness so intense, that he actually cowered beneath it and nearly dropped the phone in the grass. Something huge was passing close overhead, he sensed its immensity, could discern its vague shape suffused within that light – he squinted and strained to make it out but had to shut his eyes at the sudden flash, even more vivid than before; and when next he looked it was gone completely, whatever it had been: a trick of the moonlight refracted from the belly of the clouds; a streaking meteor; heat lightning; a host of angels delivering the chosen.

The static receded inside the phone, and his wife's voice crackled in his ear again, quieter now.

"Yes," he said, and the brittle laugh that came from him as he craned his neck to stare into the star-studded sky was full of awe. "Yes, it's *real*. It's all *true*. It really *is*."

They cried together, connected across provinces through the unreliable conduit of the phone.

After a moment, he listened to his wife clearing her throat, saying something. Voice wavering, he said, "You're welcome, honey." He listened a moment more. "Okay. I'm coming straight home. I'll see you in a couple of days."

The line was disconnected on the opposite end. He pocketed the phone and walked to his car, which was waiting along the side of the narrow farmer's road that led into the field from the distant street. He felt the overwhelming need to hold his wife, and be held by her. Briefly, he looked into the sky, found the binary stars frosting brighter than all the other celestial bodies shimmering in the blackness. And though he was crying again, his heart in that difficult moment knew a new kind of comfort, and it was a warmth against the cold night.

SOME SAW THE FIRE EXODUS

-Click-

— can't understand. Taking one's life is a right and privilege. Beating Death's angel — whoever or whatever He or She or It might have been had it been given the chance to extinguish our light — and delivering oneself into Death's arms of our own volition. We choose our own means of departure, its degree of violence or peace, so that our journey to the true place called Paradise comes as swiftly and assuredly as we wish.

Each of us makes the long journey wholly alone, yes, but we may set out on the great exodus from Pain to Paradise together. And once convened in our sanctuary, we shall remain together always, a new family of forever.

Who's with me? Let me see your hands! Let me see the fire of pain and fury and joy in your eyes! Let me see your hearts and your souls. Ah, there! There it is, my children. I see you all clearly. And so let us set out . . . now! Drink, my children! Drink the fire of our new life in the New Kingdom!

-Click-

The white-robed man had pressed the stop button on the cassette player resting on the lectern – it was an ancient model used by the school board of yesteryear that they'd found tucked into a storage cabinet alongside towers of out-dated textbooks, geometry sets, and a wooden-beaded abacus when they'd first commandeered the long-closed schoolhouse – silencing the hissing of the tape in the old amplifiers that stood on either side of the wooden stage. He looked out across the gymnasium, and the rows of his disciples sitting cross-legged on the parquet floor, their identical white robes brilliant against the drab surroundings. They numbered one hundred and twenty-five, all town locals or from the surrounding towns and villages spread throughout the Essex County area. Some he knew intimately from their regular meetings, some were strangers to him, but for their common purpose there on that most momentous of days.

The man bathed them in his smile, bittersweet, empathic, radiant. Sweat glistened on his face in the oppressive air, though his oration lost none of its wild passion.

"My children, you've heard the voice of our Father, for whose voice I act as humble vessel." He placed a hand on the cassette recorder and caressed it lovingly. "You've heard him, and I have heard you all, and brought us together, here, on this great day. Our day of salvation has finally arrived."

His followers called him the Sirius Sorcerer, for the magic he'd shown them all: peeling away the deceiving fabric of the bitter everyday – and the places of trauma from which they all came – and revealing for them the path to a better place of solace than could be found in bottles and pills and needles and endless promiscuity and other damning sins. He'd shown them the deliverance gleaming like a treasure beneath the reality they'd been shown their whole lives until coming into his nurturing care, until the New Family had taken them in and remade their dissatisfaction and pain into a new and glimmering hope while they waited for their fated, preordained day of salvation. He was a sorcerer, truly, revealing the secret un-guessed magic in the world for the few select members of their special family waiting for the exodus to commence.

The Sorcerer's lips touched the microphone, his voice carrying throughout the gymnasium to reverberate from the high ceiling. "You heard him, that great man, Michael Boreal, who loved his brave family with all his heart, and who led them on their great pilgrimage and escape to the Better Place. In fact, you all heard the call long, long ago. In the deepest place yawning like a black hole inside each of you, begging to be filled – with the goodness, with the warmth, with the light, with the peace you haven't known in so long that you can no longer quite remember it. But oh, how you all deserve it! How we all deserve peace again, from the demons who hound our hearts."

Voices cried out, echoing in the huge space:

"Hallelujah!"

"Amen, Sorcerer!"

"We're ready, Father!"

The Sorcerer smiled. Tears fell from his eyes. He raised his hands high in the sweltering air. "And so we are gathered here today, to bid goodbye to all this that we've known, and to embrace a greater tomorrow, upon a greater plane unattainable to all but the very few select, those chosen, those fortunate ones: *us!* This: our new family! I love you, brothers and sisters! I love you with all of my broken heart! With all the strength of my undying *light!* Let us be free, finally, *together!* And let us rejoice in our new freedom!"

A roar went up, filling the gymnasium like thunder. There were tears in the eyes of the people, just as tears continued to stream from the eyes of their leader.

At the rear of the gymnasium, in a row occupied by only a handful of disciples, a man and woman clung to one another. The man was looking toward the rafters of the room; he was weeping, and there was righteous ecstasy in his voice:

"Celeste, darling – mom and dad are coming home to you now. We can't wait, baby. We're coming home to you!"

He raised his hands in the air, beseechingly. The woman clutched him fiercely, weeping with abandon. Had they not been so immersed in the rapture of the moment, they might have experienced a sensation of being watched; or noticed a subtly shuddering shadow darken the narrow rectangle of sunlight that fell across them from the ajar steel door at the back of the gymnasium, propped open with a stone and forgotten, the field beyond still and hazy in the sweltering summer afternoon.

The Sorcerer raised a paper cup high in the air and, like a reflection, his followers lifted their cups, too.

"Drink, my family. *Drink!*"

As they tilted the magical transporting drink to their mouths, the small shadow silhouetted in the doorway darted away, letting the sunlight of the summer day spill more fully into that room of ecstasy.

Outside, the day burned – deep-August hot and humid, with a new tension in the air, a new electricity that silenced the birds and insects and convinced town residents to remain indoors; as if a great storm was nearly upon them, or some other thing just as colossal and beyond their control.

Alec stood at the boundary of the small back lot and the field. The old schoolhouse reared up behind him, its shadow casting a line across the field beyond which the grass was golden in the afternoon sunlight. Slowly, reluctantly, he edged closer to this boundary until he felt the sun touch his face.

There were small groups of children playing in the field stretching away before him, lost in the freedom of the day with thoughts of school not even the remotest possible annoyance in their minds. Some played a game of baseball in the dusty diamond at the far end of the field. A group of girls giggled their way through a game of hopscotch on the cement trail winding its way circuitously along one side of the field; another group, mostly boys but with a couple of tom-boy girls mixing it up in the fray, were gathered among the massive rolls of new turf that the town was in the process of planting overtop the exposed soil at the edge of the field bordering the woods to the south.

Using one of these massive pieces of turf as his throne, one boy declared to the boys tussling on the grass before him, "I am your king! You shall follow me into battle!" He was spiking a cheap plastic sword into the sky, the green faux-jewel embedded in its cross-hilt flashing in the sun. The triumphant way he brandished it and the fact that he'd brought it with him from home made it clear that the toy was dear to him.

The exuberant roars of his warrior-subjects drifted into the sky, swelling his chest. One boy threw a challenge at him from his place directly before the throne. "I shall never bow down to you! This throne is rightfully mine!" He was a tall thin boy whose immense spectacles and stooped posture gave him the appearance of an elderly man, and the crude weapon he was flourishing – a gnarled branch – might have made just as good a walking stick as a sword. He smiled a gleeful smile even as his challenge hung on the air, pleasantly oblivious to the social tortures waiting for him in the merciless halls of his secondary school career.

Alec watched this play-drama unfold with distant eyes. Had he known the children, he wouldn't have wanted to be part of their game anyways. How could he play, after what he'd witnessed through the ajar door of the schoolhouse, momentous and frightening, like a glimpse into a mysterious world he'd never heard about until his sister had confided it to him, and that he hadn't believed in – not really, not *really* – until this day.

Alec grew irritated by the jubilant cries of the kids, though mostly he was upset that she'd gone to the secret schoolhouse meeting even after he'd begged her not to. He thought of their conversation late the night before, both of them in tears as he begged her to stay, while she begged him to let her go. They'd been a rare kind of kid brother and older sister, who'd always been friends and allies, unlike their classmates who all seemed to loathe their respective siblings. Alec hadn't understood why Karen had needed to be a part of what was happening here on this day; he'd been confused about it until she'd explained it to him. He'd asked her, feeling smart and superior and confident, as if he'd found some glaring hole in her plan and that by showing it to her he'd be able to convince her to stay: she'd always claimed her boyfriend was her saviour because he understood her and shared the same experiences she had, so why then did they both want what the white-robed group was promising them – why did she need a paradise among the stars if she had her boyfriend to keep her happy?

But she'd told him, and though he hadn't admitted it to her, he'd understood. He understood that the Thing They Never Talked About, the thing that had happened to his sister two years before and changed the lives of everyone in their family, had made life too hard for her here. It had all become too much and she and her boyfriend were doing what they had to in order to get away from it. And her boyfriend, though Alec resented his special status as the centre of his sister's universe, was actually a pretty decent person to join her there. He must really love his sister to be with her inside the old gymnasium today, and wear the weird white robes and drink the magic potion. He shook his head, unable to dispel the vision of the two of them in the gymnasium, dressed in the same white robes as the others, cups in hands, like some weird hippy commune.

Alec watched the heat haze send its shimmering lines skyward, waiting in the pregnant atmosphere for the thing to happen that his sister had told him about, knowing that though all logic said that it could not, it most definitely would. And so when, a moment later, the startled cries of children rang out across the field everywhere, he wasn't surprised.

"Hey guys!" This came from the boy-king, now standing on his throne of turf and silencing his companions with the urgency in his voice, his toy sword pointing a quivering line toward the sky above the schoolhouse. *"Look!"*

The children turned to look into the sky, shielding their eyes from the sun with their hands as if they were saluting what they saw.

Alec turned helplessly to follow where they all looked, feeling unsurprised by the sight of the miracle materialized in the blue, though no less awed.

There, drifting upward, were dozens and dozens of individual flaming objects. The children, squinting in the afternoon brightness, eventually understood what it was they saw, no matter how incredible – how inconceivable – it was: people on fire, rising into the sky. The rooftop of the schoolhouse, above which the figures floated, was spitting smoke, and small fires burned here, there. Its surface was crooked, rubble-strewn, as if the people had burst up through the roof from below. The longer they watched, the more and more burning people continued to exit through the broken roof to join their companions ascending into the sky.

A moment of awe followed, during which the children watched in a collective hush as the procession of burning people climbed higher and higher. Then some cried out, excited by the vision, replying to it in the way of children in thrall to what appeared magical, without giving a second thought to the inherently darker seed of the vision.

"Look! *Look!*"

"Superheroes!"

"Whoah!"

"Space people!"

"I wanna fly, too!"

But some children saw the fiery aerial cavalcade and were stirred much more deeply by the vision. Alec turned at a frantic whispering from close by: the girl had appeared beside him, though he hadn't heard her approach. She was around his age, plump and red-faced with tears streaming down her cheeks. Her crooked blonde bangs hung over eyes that watched the sky avidly, unblinking.

"Take me with you take me with you take me with you," she was saying, over and over, as if she were reciting a prayer or spell.

Alec watched her a moment, wondering what she saw. He wondered what the vision might mean to her, for it to have such a profound effect on her, to make her weep while the children around her were only giddy with excitement. If he hadn't felt the way he did then – if it wasn't his sister and best friend leaving him – he might have spoken to the girl, and asked her what it was about the fiery spectacle that made her so sad. He had a feeling they could be good friends. Maybe they shared some common thing, a loved one leaving them, or a desire to go with them because of some specific darkness in their days that made summer vacations feel like anything but an escape. Maybe he and this girl were members of the same tribe and together they'd be stronger than they could be as individual pieces of the great puzzle of the universe.

He might have tried articulating these complicated-sounding things to the girl but he didn't. He only turned to watch the vision again himself.

The spectacle of the burning people had dwindled with distance, eventually becoming lost in the depths of the sky; the one hundred twenty-five disciples of the Saviour Michael Boreal and the vessel of his voice, the Sirius Sorcerer, disappeared into the summer sky, journeying into the heart of the twin stars where a promise lay waiting for them.

The children maintained their sky-vigil even when parents, alerted by neighbours to the occurrence of some sort of ominous event, came seeking their sons and daughters and urged them to come home. Alec continued watching the sky too, imagining his sister in the place she'd described to him even as the sound of sirens and adults' voices invaded the earlier quiet of the park, creating a bedlam in which thoughts of everlasting peace became difficult to contemplate. And he kept watching even when the policemen bustled across the parking lot to investigate some mysterious and alarming incident that had reportedly taken place inside the old abandoned schoolhouse burning in the summer sunshine.

Alec, eyes fixed on the sky, made his declaration quietly but adamantly, feeling the truth of it in his heart even as tears stung his eyes and made a molten stain of the sun:

"Karen: I *will* see you again."

When he felt the fingers of the girl standing beside him slip inside his own he said nothing, only held on.

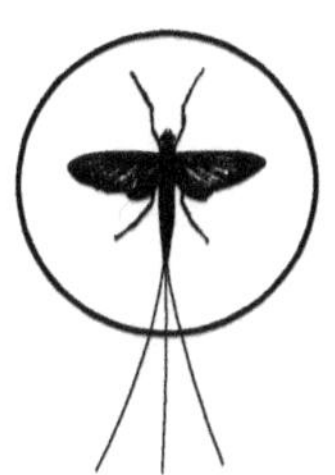

THE MAYFLIES
WANT TO FLY

The blood puddle was dark in the dust. Black like oil but thicker somehow. It reflected the sun hanging overhead as a luminous, nebulous smear. It reminded the boy of a window descending into deep, forbidding places. He stared a while into its depths, mesmerized. He was weary. His body ached. His skeleton bowed earthwards. He felt the pain in his bones. He'd been digging all day and could dig no more. He could never dig like this again.

He looked to her standing beside him, leaning on her own shovel. She looked every inch a goddess, resplendent in the bright air. He was grateful for her strength in the sapping temperature. He felt that perhaps if he stared at her long enough, then maybe some of her strength might seep its way into him, too. Her cheeks were flushed with the heat of the mid-day hour or the fierceness of her spirit, like Athena bathed in sunlight. Her eyes were incongruous in her molten features, serene and icy as she scanned first the willow trees' sagging arms that enfolded the small clearing, beyond which murmured the western horizon of the 401 snaking into the shimmering distance; and then sweeping her gaze eastwards, where farmers' fields stretched flat and endless, their barrenness dotted with telephone poles like crosses marking the miles. Crow's feet made neat little parentheses around her eyes but still she radiated youthfulness and vigor as she surveyed the burning landscape.

She felt his scrutiny. She turned, slowly, as if from a daze or daydream, and smiled a remote smile. Her eyes sparkled. She'd left her cheap plastic sunglasses burning on the dashboard – she braved the blinding day with her naked stare. She turned back to the ground before them and kicked dirt onto the blood marking the site of their off-road stop. He helped with his hands, cupping handfuls of soil and stones and dropping them into the black pool like an offering or sacrifice, a funereal gesture without words spoken or prayers delivered.

She pulled something from her bag. Sunlight flashed from it, reminding him that his toil was not yet done. He could do this, he told himself, tightening his grip on the shovel's handle and steeling himself for the remaining labor. He could yet dig one final pit in the ground. He slammed the spade's metal tip downwards. Pain stabbed his shoulders and callused hands. He dug this remaining hole, much smaller than the other, in silence punctuated by occasional groans of exertion. She'd insisted on this digging of dual holes, because no one, she maintained – not even the worst of people – should spend eternity with an artifact of darkness like this.

When he was finished, he leaned heavily on the shovel, blinking sweat from his vision. The voice of the highway drifted unabated from the distance. He watched her as she dropped the pistol into the gaping hole. He filled it quickly, to the queer accompanying image that flitted into his straying thoughts, of a person's mouth being stuffed with rags. She helped him pat down the mound of earth, kicking a camouflage of branches overtop it.

His vision was uncertain. The willow trees swayed before him. She saw his great fatigue and came to him. She held him close. She didn't mind his sweat-bathed limbs and stench. Leaning from him a moment later, she watched him closely. Her words were vehement, a hot wind on his face. "It's done. It's done. Now we can go."

They left the secluded roadside area, weaving between the scrub brush and returning to the car nestled among the hanging willow trees. What bags of theirs that hadn't fit into the trunk lay scattered in the rear. They clambered in, the vehicle dappled in sunlight filtering through the roof of foliage overhead. She nosed the car forward over the grass and dirt. A moment later, they turned into the road once more and drove for the sun bleeding into the horizon.

*

The motel room was tiny. It smelled stale and its air was stifling. The walls were stained in places, and the ceiling, too. He'd found stains in the sheets, as well – faded yellow continents marking the place of others' past unions in the bed. He looked to her, clothed in a light sleeveless shirt and cut-off denims, the oven air cloying and heavy as a tangible thing. Sweat darkened the cotton between her small breasts. It glistened on her arms and legs and pooled in the narrow cleft between her collarbones. He shone with it, too, his ebony skin lustrous. His limbs felt boneless, numb and impossible to lift from the clinging bed sheets.

They lay a while without words, sharing the bed although a second bed haunted the opposite corner, forlorn-looking. The ceiling fan warbled uncertainly in the centre of the shabby room, churning the heavy atmosphere. He thought distantly of the times he'd been given kitchen duty, helping the orphanage cook by stirring his viscous soups or lard-laden tubs with a long wooden ladle. The image flitted away and his head seemed empty. Beside him, a fly annoyed her ear and he watched from the corner of his eye as she absently batted it into other orbits.

Concern returned to haunt him, and he dared the indolent peace of the moment with words. "Where are we going? We've been ghosting the county all day . . ." he drifted off. The words fell heavily from his tongue. He heard the uncertainty in his voice. He felt his youthfulness then, the way he hadn't felt it when she'd paid for the room an hour before and he'd waited outside like a grown-up guarding their belongings in the parking lot. He could only lay motionless, sweating and awaiting her answer.

She watched the ceiling a moment before speaking. "We're headed someplace. We're . . . reaching for an empyrean. Little by little, we're going to get there."

Ironically, outside of her classroom, he was no longer shy about his ignorance while in her presence. "I don't know what that means."

"You do. Deep down, you do," she assured him enigmatically. She turned to him. Her eyes were gentle looking into his. She curled her fingers into a flaccid fist, which she placed against his chest.

They lay in silence for a time and she said, "We aren't doing anything wrong. We haven't done anything wrong. No one knows, besides. No one will find out."

It was as though she could hear the worries that fluttered inside of his skull. She was uncanny like this. She'd always been this way. The only person who had ever taught him things, whether meaningful lessons uncovered inside of school books, or revelations about the thoughts and urges of the people he saw every day. He believed the certainty in her voice, though. He exhaled the breath he'd pent up without realizing it. Her voice lingered in his ears, and he wondered if she could hear the echo of what she'd said, too. The way she'd spoken it was magical, like a spell that acted as a calming element inside the raging storm of him: *We* aren't doing anything wrong. He believed her. It was a comfort then. It was better than music then. It was better than the words in books. He felt his heart beat gentler behind his sweaty chest. The pulse throbbed a gentler song in his temple, too.

He thought of blood, in the dust, in the fabric of the clothes of strangers, staining his hands like an emblem of wickedness and righteousness.

The air in the room was oppressive, but eventually they slept.

"You have nice skin. Like chocolate. Dark chocolate."

She told him this while examining his profile in the driver's seat. She liked letting him drive. He enjoyed the freedom of feigning full-fledged adulthood and she relished the opportunity to stretch her limbs and close her eyes and watch the sun-glow through her weary eyelids. He was a year shy of legal driving age but they both knew he needed no certificate to ghost the roads they travelled. They'd earned these privileges in other ways that bound them to the highway.

Silence reigned over the moon-drenched glade.

They'd discovered the willow grove while seeking an adequate site to break for the night. Nosing the car gingerly through the scrub brush and wild grass; weaving between the overhanging willows, the silhouettes of their sagging arms looking mournful in the silver light. Rolling through the copse into the unexpected open air of the glade, bathed in celestial luminescence.

The night was moderately less muggy than the preceding day, nearly cool. It was a kiss of relief on his bare arms. The sky was a star field everywhere he searched. It was a grand picture. Colossal and seemingly significant. He wanted to say something about this but feared his voice would shatter the perfect stillness.

He turned to her beside him where they lay on the car hood, sipping ice-cold colas. Her eyes were glazed and far away. He wanted to bring her to him. He braved the quiet, but softly. "What do you think about stars? You think there's anyone out there, like some people say?"

She watched the sky a while, her gaze unchanged.

"No."

Unequivocal, and assured, her familiar lecturing manner, but wholly different in the way she no longer seemed to see romance in the vistas she witnessed. Her eyes lingered there a while longer, though. They looked calm, blue and icy. She sparkled in the silver air. He said nothing more to move the scene.

"Look at the spaces between them," she murmured then, sounding more teacherly than ever, the way that comforted him most. "All the negative space. Maybe it's the final darkness, coming for us all one day. Maybe we'll become a race of moles. This could be in store for us."

"For . . . *us?*" His voice carried genuine fear, and he cringed a little at its presence, so conspicuous.

"For all of us."

"That sounds scary." He ruminated on this. Then, "Can I have a smoke?"

"You really shouldn't," she said, removing the pack from her jeans pocket and passing it to him.

They lay there a while, watching the stars. Crickets played all around them. Mosquitoes flitted on the still air. The great fear came upon him, as it had been visiting him lately. He wondered whether she realized his youth, after everything they'd experienced together. He startled the silence. "I hate people. I fucking hate them all."

She looked to him. Wan lunar light made the tears beading his cheeks luminescent. Her eyes softened. She watched him a while. Her gaze hardened. Her hand found his and gripped him warmly. She returned her attention to the stars. She lifted an arm skywards, pointing. "There," she whispered softly. "Do you see them? In the east? The bright pair?"

He wiped at his eyes, ashamed. He scanned the heavens. He found the trembling stars, huge and like specks of ice. "I see them."

"Let's go there. In case they're good places. Okay?"

It was something he might have said, before. It was a romantic notion he would have hid from schoolmates and friends for fear of their derision. He felt closer to her than ever before. He admired the snowflakes burning in the east, wondering if people or angels might live there.

He removed a cigarette from the pack he clutched in sweaty fingers, and placed it between his trembling lips. He made no move to light it, and together they watched the east until their weariness urged them into the car. They spent the night there, she in the driver's seat, he curled among their luggage in the rear, the car like a giant crib nestled among the wild willow garden, the top rolled down and letting the full and immense night in with them.

*

Driving.

Miles flitting by beneath their wheels. Dust and clouds and sun and the first appearance of a gibbous moon and the first few thousand stars bathing the countryside in ethereal light.

A second moon rising suddenly from the roadside shrubbery: she turning the car towards the flickering motel sign like a beacon for their aching bodies and weary thoughts.

He plucked a mayfly gently from her bare shoulder and blew it into the night.

The motel boasted a narrow, uncertain-looking balcony which ran the length of the small, two-floor building. They leaned against the rust-eaten, rickety railing, looking out into the gravel parking lot and dense thicket beyond. The forlorn-looking car was parked directly below them.

He murmured, sleepily, "We must have travelled lots of miles, eh?"

She nodded, smoking her cigarette. Her eyes watched the distance pensively. She seemed a treasure chest whose lock remained fast. He yearned for the time when he might bathe in the opulence she held inside.

He ventured, "You taught mathematics be-fore, too, eh? You're the math wizard. Figure the numbers – how far have we gone?"

"Very, very far," she answered, and she left it at that, puffing languidly on her cigarette.

Beneath them, a couple exited the motel and drifted across the lot to their car. Retrieving some bags from the trunk, they made their way back a moment later, casting long shadows behind them. They heard the couple's door whisper closed beneath their feet. A moment passed.

"Where should we go now?" he asked tremulously.

After some rumination, she said, "We'll continue east. I've always wanted to live in a small town. There are plenty in the east. Small, quiet places. Peaceful and mellow." She put out her cigarette, squashing its flaming tip against the railing and dropping it still smouldering into the lot below.

He followed its descent. "It looks like a dying firefly."

She rubbed his arm and gave him a drawn smile. "You were always a poet. From the first day of class."

He thought back to a September so far distant it may have been another age entirely. He recalled too the way her lessons, directed to the entire thirty-plus listless students, seemed really to have only ever been for him alone – her eyes lingering on his from time to time, the way they never seemed to rest on anyone else sleepy at their small desk; the way that she invariably chose him for after-school honours of blackboard-cleaning and textbook gathering, as if she sensed his inclinations towards books and songs and other gentle ways of passing his time. He remembered the feeling of privilege that had filled him when she'd chosen him to remain after class the first time; sending him into the cramped room of maps with arms laden, the way she'd joined him there after a while, too; at first simply watching him from the doorway with a sad gaze, and then closing the door behind her and melting into his awkward arms while the hundreds of tightly-wound paper and canvas tubes towered around them on all sides like some queer wilderness shielding them from the eyes of all those living outside its dense tree-line divide. Her words had calmed his great anxiety in that strange moment: "I'm lonely, too. It's okay. It's okay." As if she could hear his thoughts, the deepest-buried, the most clandestine feelings he kept to himself and dared to share with no one.

He recalled those young days of their strange, blooming friendship with a pang of bittersweet nostalgia. A memory arrived unbidden – a morning months and months before when she'd revealed a deep part of herself to him. "I can't teach them," she'd said flatly as the remaining children drifted from the classroom, tossing a nub of chalk clatteringly at the blackboard where it ricocheted and fell to the classroom tiles in fragments. "I don't want to try to teach anyone anything ever again. Except for you. You're different from the children here. From the county people I've met. You choose to spend your time with Greek heroes and poems. You don't have cruel eyes. You and I are a pair of rare birds."

Hearing her say that made him yearn to embrace her, to hold her and be held by her like they'd done once before already, that secret moment he daydreamed of so often, when they'd been lost together among the maps of the world; then suddenly he'd started thinking of the classmates and fellow orphans of whom she was speaking, so different from him despite their common bond of abandonment in the world. Bird-shooting and schoolyard-brawling, those cussing reprobate boys, while he chose to hide in county trees with books and binoculars with which to watch and befriend birds. Disappearing from the sight of these children for fear of the wrath they might deliver him for his very dissimilarity. *I can't teach them*, she'd divulged, words like a gift for him to recite like a prayer and coax strength from when he needed it most. Because he never had been able to fathom them either, the war-like children hurling stones at each other and cursing their ugly or visibly weak classmates with spiteful words. Before her, he'd come to understand, he'd never really known anyone.

He shook his head. Thoughts like these veered too close to hazard. He wanted freedom from the wickedness he'd seen in the eyes of others. He refocused his thoughts, clearing away sinister notions so that he could consider the immediacy of the clammy night around him, the cloying smell of fast food and garbage mingling into a single noxious reek wafting from the motel's open windows and the large metal garbage dumpster in the lot below. He thought of these immediate things but, looking to the spot where her cigarette still blazed its tiny ember like a vestige of life in the midnight parking lot, he thought once again of dying creatures. He wondered what a firefly might feel if it witnessed a dying brother or sister, watching it fall to its death like a miniature star, to lay pulsing its last in a concrete lot laid down by men's hands and encroaching on their little remaining shred of wilderness.

He watched the dying cigarette in the lot below but saw a doomed insect pulse its final pulse, and become extinguished forever.

He turned and admired her profile, slim-nosed, small-chinned. He wondered if he'd ever completely fathom her and her strange, strong ways. He noticed another secret stowaway on her and picked up the mayfly between his long, nimble fingers. It had been nestled behind her ear, amid her lush hair which she let down from a pony-tail only at nights. He examined it in the moon glow, its thin wings like gossamer, its pallid, nearly translucent body undulating madly on the air as it sought fruitlessly to escape his gentle grasp. He leaned over the rail and blew the insect from his palm and into the sultry air.

They watched it flutter away into darkness. She assessed its flight, teacherly and wise once again, and more poetically than he could ever:

"It only wants to fly. It's perfect."

He turned to go back indoors. He noticed that she'd been watching him rather than the flight of the mayfly. He smiled bashfully, and gestured for her to enter before him, gentlemanly.

Inside, they watched television in the soft orange lamp glow. Nearly asleep but not quite, he heard her creak the bed and turn out the lamp, plunging the room into darkness. For some reason that he was too tired to consider, he smiled in the final blackness before his weariness took him away.

He dreamed the dream of blood and dust and blinding sunlight. When he awoke, he was bathed in sweat. Fear gripped him in the dream's wake, until the tinkling sound of water running in the bathroom drifted to him and he knew she was there with him, washing the dust of miles from her body.

He cracked open his eyelids to morning light seeping through the tattered blinds shielding the windows. He welcomed its viciousness, and despaired of the forthcoming night when the old dream would return, as it reliably did whenever sleep came for him.

They left while dawn had begun to light the east.

She led the way to the car, her steps fleet and sure. He followed, groggy with another night of fitful sleep behind him. He clambered in beside her, suddenly conscious of the rumble in his stomach.

"We'll grab some breakfast on the road," she said, awakening the car into sputtering life, a rabid sound in the stillness of the hour.

The car rolled along the driveway towards the road. He winced at the million popping sounds as the vehicle's tires crushed the mayflies clinging to the tarmac everywhere. Their marine stink haunted the air, and it made him vaguely nauseous.

She must have sensed his revulsion, or felt it herself and soldiered on despite it. "It can't be helped," she said firmly, yet with a suggestion of apology in her wincing eyes trained on the road ahead. "They're everywhere."

Her words hung between them. Another lesson seemed to dwell in them but he was too weary to consider it then. He decided to ponder it throughout the forthcoming day of dust and sun and miles behind them.

*

He happened to be watching her surreptitiously when it happened and in this way discovered that even goddesses falter. He'd seen her brow furrow, her eyes squint in indecision or maybe only anticipation of a collision she'd resigned herself to from the moment its potentiality had arisen.

He'd appeared like an apparition from the corn rows. His stride sure as he entered the road, and belying his haggard, dusty-cheeked countenance; the young man, bare-chested with his shirt hanging like a tail from the pocket of his grimy jeans, with the dull grey steel bucket in one fist and a long slender fishing pole in the other.

It felt to him as though she might have accelerated the car or perhaps it had been the day hastening them towards the inevitability of their violent meeting with the man. They ran him down. His body flew away from the car hood like a sack laden with wheat, heavily and without resistance.

They drove onwards without pause. His heart was a cacophony behind his chest. He found the man in the side mirror. He'd come to rest near the road's centre, floppy with lifelessness, like a scarecrow stationed in the street to ward off wicked travellers. The dust cloud that had followed them since they set out that morning was settling over him like a pall. Possibly it was a fitting place for him to come to rest, the boy rationalized frantically. Perhaps it was the fate he deserved. No person deserved less, possibly. These thoughts hounded him while he took turns watching the dwindling corpse in the mirror and her chiseled, stoic-looking profile beside him.

They drove without speaking for most of the afternoon. Corn country gave way to wheat seas and then barren plains of what appeared to be wholly un-tillable soil, punctuated everywhere with grey bedrock peering through the earth like hints of a subterranean civilization. Toward early evening, she spoke. "Who knows what he might have become. Goddamn them all."

The bloodlight of sunset drenched them. He nodded along to her words, to their meaning and justification, to their hard uncompromising rhythm while the stifling air whipped in through the open windows to lash his clothes and sting his skin. He'd thought that she might be thinking such things. He'd guessed and hoped this since miles back. They drove on. Her face remained hard, her eyes severe. She reminded him of a statue. A sculpture of a goddess withstanding the tenacious heat of the day, and the events held in its molten, endless hours.

A few miles later, she pulled into a wooded cul-de-sac. She silenced the engine. She placed her head on the burning wheel and wept. He watched her. He didn't know what else he might do. He tried to hold her eventually but wasn't strong enough to lift her from her despair. She only wept, her limbs flaccid and unmoving from her sides. He examined the trees about them. More willows and others whose names he didn't know. Dappling them in the final sunlight and making fluttering late afternoon shadows on the car hood and his arms, and on her shuddering beside him. He noticed the carcass of a possum lying rigid in its final death-pose a few meters away. He considered that it might be roadkill, too, and had crawled here, with what lingering life it had possessed, to die in the peace of the woods. To become stippled prettily in sunshine rather than lie exposed and burning in the sun-scorched road. One of the animal's eyes, he saw, seemed to stare in their direction, as if transfixed by the scene of them convened there in the cemetery stillness, too.

She sobbed without respite for many minutes. When she was finished, she didn't speak as he'd hoped she would. She only restarted the engine into coughing, chugging life, and took them onto the road once more.

The boy grew sleepy in the residual sunlight. The bloody scarecrow haunting the road and the glade's frozen possum were like different chapters of a dream they'd left behind them.

Later that night, lying beside her on the motel room's narrow sodden mattress, he dared to ask.

"Will they catch us for what we done?"

Her voice was gentle. "No, baby."

Bolstered by his boldness in asking the question, he ventured, "Will they catch us for the other thing?"

Her answer came quickly, heatedly in the darkness of the room. "*Never.*"

They lay in silence a while. His thoughts grew uncertain with his weariness. She rolled toward him. Her smell of sweat and dust and sunlight awakened him a little from his torpor. She murmured sleepily, "Rest. Rest. Even Perseus needed rest. The morning will be easier." He believed her. He never questioned her. She knew everything. They were the luckiest pair of birds, as she'd claimed herself, to have found each other in the trackless miles of the world.

The highway had gathered them into its endless track at dawn and by near-dusk still they rocketed into the east. Another long day of driving with few stops along the way. Few words between them marked the final miles of their passage. They'd rolled the car's roof down, as they preferred to ride from time to time when the humidity was so vicious that simple open windows wouldn't suffice to keep them cooled off. He read a little from his cache of battered paperbacks. He flipped idly through a magazine or two. Mostly he watched

58

the countryside of cows and fields and occasional barns racing past. Her eyes were pensive and fixed on the road unwinding before them. A simple cycle had developed, mellow and serene in the hurtling midst of their highway travel. Drive and drive, roadside lulls for relieving themselves or eating at roadside diners or cafes, and drive and drive more. He considered this pattern of forward motion, relentless yet mellow in its monotony. It had its calming qualities. He could grow accustomed to driving through towns and cities and never really stopping again.

Then, suddenly, they were spinning.

The sudden transformation was colossal, from the uniformity of languid afternoon momentum to the shocking squealing of brakes and screeching of tires and violent vertigo throwing their bowels into disarray. Things flew from the car; suitcases, bags, books, loose articles of clothing, pens, scraps of paper, cassettes, sunglasses, cigarette packs and lighters, paper cups. They would have flown too but for their safety belts pinioning them against their seats, battling the chaos of gravity. He screamed shrilly. She cursed vehemently. They felt one side of the vehicle lifting from the tarmac in their headlong flight. Kaleidoscopes of western and eastern and northern and southern landscapes took turns flitting before their revolving vision. He thought of a roller coaster he'd ridden as a boy. He thought of Death rising from the earth and coming for them. Then they clenched their eyes closed tightly as the dying afternoon sun spun ever more violently, violently.

He remembered that afternoon's brightness. A glare he hadn't known was possible to exist in the world. It had seemed apocalyptic as he'd stood in the schoolyard abutting the orphanage, unable to speak, able only to watch her with the girl in her arms. Like a goddess come down from above to bless the Earth with her presence, she was, to hold the crumbling girl-child in her ivory arms. He'd looked, startled, where the young girl's blood made vivid geographies on her white dress. It streaked her bare caramel knees and calves obscenely, too. She wailed and he thought the primal, anguished sound of her would tear his body apart. He was unable to look from the scene in the yard, though. He marveled at the goddess' strength in the midst of such potent pain. All the pain in the world seemed gathered into the child's cries, and still the goddess held her relentlessly while his own stomach revolted from her mewling voice and his eyes wished to rebel and look to easier places. The other children were stunned into silent immobility, too, bewitched by the vision of suffering unlike any calamity they'd witnessed before.

The girl eventually grew quiet and still in her arms.

It had been his sister weeping in the goddess' embrace. She was gone then, having exited the soft shell of her body and flown elsewhere. He knew this, somehow, watching her small limp body in his teacher's arms. The teenagers who had taken her into the thin copse abutting the orphanage had vanished somewhere into the terrible heart of the day. They had made him realize for the first time that the Devil walked the same paths that he did every day.

His teacher, the goddess, looked up. He saw her eyes. Through her tears, they were new. She had emerged from her weaker shell, too, like he had, a new creature. The descended goddess watched the boy evenly, as though he was worthy of her scrutiny, despite his cowardice which had urged him, the only family his sister had in the world, to want to look away from her in her final moments on Earth. Everything was changed, he realized. Himself and his teacher and the day and the world in which he and she lived. He sensed it, underneath the great weight of his sorrow and numbness.

Vengeance would be introduced into his world.

A new epoch had begun.

*

The stink of burned rubber filled their nostrils. A dust cloud hung over the scene. In it they watched the grizzled, mangy-looking dog pad across the highway. Its muzzle hung low to the burning tarmac, its tongue lolled lethargically. Its moist eyes beheld them. They were mournful, pained almost.

They watched the procession cross the narrow strip of the highway like a miracle given up by the afternoon. The mutt led, and the others followed: second in the formation was a kitten, frail and grey-furred and with wobbly big-pawed steps; next came the raccoon, lumbering and with a furtive glare delivered them in their stilled car; and then a waddling goose and its troop of goslings like bobbing yellow tennis balls; and then a pair of large lavender butterflies skimming erratically over the burning road like two gossamer veils borne on the zephyr-like breeze. Next, a deer crossed the pavement with delicate and deliberate steps, looking both ways, head raised high to smell for danger, antlers both majestic and deadly-looking. Lastly padded a coyote, the rearguard of the group, eyeing them suspiciously with emerald, sentinel's eyes of mystery as it passed through the settling dust before the stilled vehicle. Mayflies fluttered everywhere, following in the air over the procession like a host of frenzied guardian angels.

They sat amazed in their seats. The dust settled a new coat of grime on them.

"This is the world," she said, her voice hushed, awed, reverential. "Nobody could ever tame it."

They watched the procession file across the road, ascend the incline of the adjacent ditch, and begin a slow trudge across the fields.

The boy's vision swam. His shirt clung to him like skin. He blinked but the mirage remained, moving determinedly across the uneven earth. Breathless, he still managed to speak, in a voice of wonder. "You stopped for them."

She nodded. The heat was formidable. Sweat beaded her forehead. A drop fell from her upper lip, flashing like a tiny jewel in the sun.

They stood in their seats, shielding their eyes with their hands and following the animals' progress until they were a ghostly impression in the distant heat-haze. Perhaps it had indeed been a mirage urged from the wild grass and concrete by the formidable heat. Another delirium like scarecrow men and other bloody roadside ghosts.

The boy looked overhead, seeking to clear his thoughts. The afternoon sky had given way to a near-dusk striated panorama of magenta and deepening crimson. The sun had dipped across the sky. It was set to scald the treetops in the west. He felt hollow. He needed to be filled. The heat had baked him dry. The days had burned the joy from him.

Bravery or foolishness impelled his words into the heavy air.

"Will you be my mother?"

She turned to him. They stood in their seats, watching each other through the swirling dust. Her smile gave him his answer, and the water welling in her eyes as they washed over him trembling at her side.

He groaned his seat's leather as he leaned toward her. He kissed her burning cheek. By way of gratitude for all of her lessons, and because he loved the feel of her. She kissed his cheek in return. Her lips were like fire. She felt good on his skin. She refreshed him somehow in the sapping languor of the day. She gave him the strength to continue through the remaining hours and miles and dust clouds awaiting them. He wished that they would live forever, in their endless moment.

Soon, they clambered back into their places. She focused her red-rimmed eyes on the road before them. He watched as she pressed her small bare foot down on the gas pedal. She urged them forward again, slowly, conjuring a new dust ghost to follow in their wake. They gathered speed. They roared through the stifling near-twilight, crossing town borders and beating time in their vehicle like a speeding bullet. Their lost luggage they left behind in the road, like offerings at the site of their day's most important moment. The wind whipped through their hair. Her sizzling kiss lingered on his cheek. He suddenly felt free of something in the embrace of the fiery day. He suddenly felt cared for, and safer than he'd ever been before, and no longer hollow at all.

He understood it at last, in the velocity and certainty of the moment. A pair of stars was shimmering in the east like a mirror of themselves, awaiting the onset of full dark to reveal their snowy promise.

Together, they would reach a new place.

When your Earth-mud walls are scaled at last,
strike out: your home waits in the vault
None of it was your fault

We belong somewhere, too.

- the Deathray Bradburys, "Migration of the
Ancient Children"
(a lost song recovered from a live bootleg cassette
recording, source unknown)

About the Author

Alexander Zelenyj is the author of the books
Blacker Against the Deep Dark,
Songs for the Lost, ***Experiments At 3 Billion
A.M.***, and ***Black Sunshine***. He lives in Windsor,
Ontario, Canada with his wife and their
menagerie of animals.